COUNTRIES IN THE NEWS

GERMANY

Kieran Walsh

Rourke

Publishing LLC

Vero Beach, Florida 32964

www.rourkepublishing.com

The country's flag is correct at the time of going to press.

PHOTO CREDITS: ©Joerg Koch/AFP/Getty Images Cover
©ArtToday, Inc. pg 11;©Benjamin Schulte pg 18;
All other images ©Peter Langer Associated Media Group

Title page: *The Rhine River is well known for its appealing scenery.*

Editor: Frank Sloan

Cover and interior design by Nicola Stratford

Library of Congress Cataloging-in-Publication Data

Walsh, Kieran.
  Germany / Kieran Walsh.
    p. cm. -- (Countries in the news II)
  Includes bibliographical references and index.
  ISBN 1-59515-173-7 (hardcover)
  1. Germany--Juvenile literature. I. Title. II. Series: Walsh, Kieran. Countries in the news
II.
  DD17.W35 2004
  943--dc22
                                    2004009683

Printed in the USA

CG/CG

TABLE OF CONTENTS

WELCOME TO
GERMANY

Germany is a country in northern Europe. Most of Germany is **landlocked**, though parts of the country do come into contact with the North and Baltic seas.

Traditional houses abound in the south of Germany.

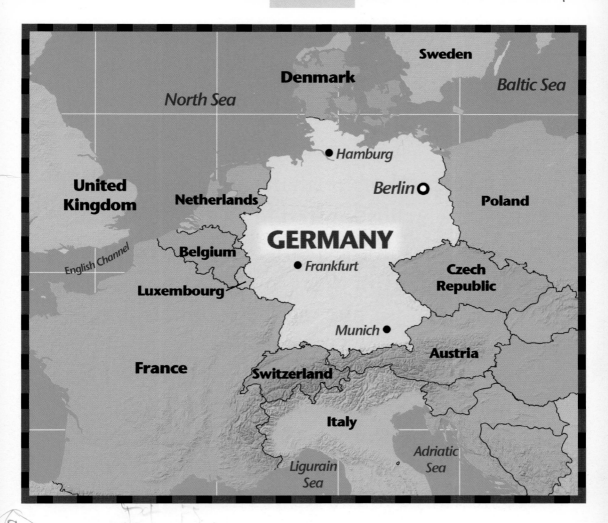

Germany is **approximately** the size of the state of Montana. The population of Germany is roughly 83 million. If that sounds like a lot of people for a fairly small country, you're right.

Germany has the second highest population in Europe.

The capital of Germany and its largest city is Berlin, which is located in eastern Germany. However, up until 1999, the capital of Germany was Bonn, a city in western Germany.

The reason for moving the capital is that, until very recently, Germany had been split into two countries. After World War II (1939-1945), Germany was divided into East and West Germany. The Russians were given the east, and the **Allies** (Americans, British, and French) were in charge of the west. The city of Berlin was also divided, although it was located in East Germany. This situation held until 1989, when the Berlin Wall was torn down, and the country was **reunified**.

After 1989, people chipped away to get rid of the Berlin Wall.

THE PEOPLE

About 92 percent of the people living in Germany were also born there. The remaining 8 percent come from other countries, including Turkey, the former Yugoslavia, and Italy. Many of these immigrants are **gastarbeiter**, meaning guest workers.

These old buildings are in a section of Frankfurt.

Street musicians are a common sight all over Germany.

About 85 percent of Germans live in cities like Berlin, Hamburg, Munich, and Frankfurt. Although German cities are crowded, there is little crime compared to most of Europe.

The two major religious groups in Germany are Protestant and Roman Catholic. For the most part, Protestants tend to live in the north of Germany and Roman Catholics live in the south.

Neuschwanstein Castle in southern Germany

A view of the cathedral at Cologne, from across the Rhine River.

Like the United States, Germany is a very modern country. Most people own television sets, cars, and computers. Although the birth rate is low, Germany's population has a life expectancy of 77 years.

LIFE IN GERMANY

Even though most of the German population lives in cities, Germans spend much of their free time enjoying their beautiful countryside. Germans are hard workers, but they also have about eight weeks of vacation every year.

The Rhine River provides spectacular views of the German countryside.

A street in Hameln, in north central Germany

Germany's terrain is composed of lush green forests and winding rivers like the Rhine and the Danube. Weather in Germany is mild. During the summer months, temperatures are around 75° F (24° C.)—perfect weather for being outdoors.

SCHOOL AND SPORTS

Nine years of schooling is the **minimum** requirement for German children. Despite the fact that German is the **official** language, many Germans can speak another language, and frequently this is English.

As with most of Europe, soccer is the most popular sport in Germany. Hiking, biking, and skiing are other popular sports that take advantage of Germany's varied landscape.

Bicycle riders enjoy a snack in a park in Hannover.

Schoolchildren in Berlin

The **literacy** rate in Germany is 99%

FOOD AND HOLIDAYS

Traditional German food is often a **variation** on two items—meat and potatoes. Meats include several varieties of **wurst**, or sausage. Potatoes can be found in many forms. Perhaps the most popular is the **rosti**, a fried potato pancake. Another German favorite is sauerkraut, which is a kind of cooked cabbage. Many of these foods can be eaten at an **imbiss**, or outdoor food stand.

Christmas markets are very popular in Germany. These markets usually open toward the end of November and stay in business until Christmas Eve. At Christmas markets people can buy toys, cookies, and ornaments.

There are plenty of items for sale in this Christmas market.

A relatively new holiday in Germany is the Love Parade, which has been in existence since 1989. This parade takes place each July and celebrates peace and music.

The main square in the city of Munich

THE FUTURE OF GERMANY

For the past few years, Germany has been in a **recession**. Its economy has had the slowest growth rate of all countries in the European Union. The German government, though, is working hard to correct this situation.

The German people are intelligent and **resourceful**. As they have in the past, they will overcome their current problems, and Germany will remain an important and powerful country.

Flea markets are a popular sight in many German cities and towns.

FAST FACTS

Area: 137,846 square miles (356,994 sq km)

Borders: Netherlands, Belgium, Luxembourg, and France to the west, Switzerland and Austria in the south, and Poland and the Czech Republic to the east and north. To the north, Germany borders Denmark and comes into contact with the Baltic and North seas

Population: 82,398,326
Monetary Unit: The euro
Largest Cities: Berlin, Hamburg, Munich, Cologne, Frankfurt
Government: Federal Republic

Religions: Protestant, Roman Catholic, Islam
Crops: Potatoes, wheat, barley, sugar beets, fruit, cabbages

Natural Resources: Iron ore, coal, timber, uranium, copper, salt
Major Industries: Machinery, electronics, shipbuilding, textiles, iron, cement

THE EURO

In January 2002, Germany was one of 12 European countries that started using the euro as its official **currency**. Up until then, Germany's currency was the **Deutsche mark**.

The euro was created for the benefit of people living in Austria, Belgium, Finland, France, Germany, Greece, Ireland, Italy, Luxembourg, the Netherlands, Portugal, and Spain. Now, residents of these countries can travel and purchase goods without having to use different forms of money.

The fabled university town of Heidelberg

GLOSSARY

Allies (AL EYES) — People who united to fight a war

approximately (uh PROKS uh mut lee) — about; roughly

currency (KUR un see) — a form of money

Deutsche mark (DOY chuh MARK) — Germany's money before the euro

gastarbeiter (GAH ster BITE ur) — German word meaning guest workers

imbiss (IM buss) — an outdoor food stand, a kind of snack bar

landlocked (LAND LOKT) — bordered only by land rather than water

literacy (LIT er uh see) — the ability to read and write

minimum (MIN uh mem) — the least amount possible or allowed

official (uh FISH uhl) — accepted, favored

recession (re SESH un) — a period of poor economic development

resourceful (re SORS ful) — clever; using available skills or goods

reunified (ree YOU nuh fyd) — brought together again

rosti (REST ee) — a type of cooked potato

variation (var ee AY shun) — a different version of something

wurst (VOORST) — sausage

FURTHER READING

Find out more about Germany with these helpful books:

- Ayer, Eleanor H. *Germany (Modern Nations of the World)*. Lucent Books, 2001

- Blashfield, Jean F. *Enchantment of the World: Germany*. Children's Press, 2003

- Bramwell, Martyn. *The World in Maps: Europe*. Lerner Publications, 2000

- Schanz, Sonjua. *The Changing Face of Germany*. Raintree/Steck Vaughn, 2003

- Zuehlke, Jeffrey. *Visual Geography: Germany in Pictures*. Lerner Publications, 2003

WEBSITES TO VISIT

- www.infoplease.com/ipa/A0107568.html
  Infoplease – Germany

- www.germany-info.org/relaunch/info/missions/embassy/embassy.html
  German Embassy – Washington, D.C.

INDEX

About the Author

Kieran Walsh is a writer of children's nonfiction books, primarily on historical and social studies topics. Walsh has been involved in the children's book field as editor, proofreader, and illustrator as well as author.